Lost in the Snow

Lost in the Snow

Holly Webb

Illustrated by Sophy Williams

SCHOLASTIC INC.

New York Toronto London Auckland Sydney
Mexico City New Delhi Hong Kong Buenos Aires

For Sammy and Marble,
and for the original Rosie

ISBN-13: 978-0-545-20273-2
ISBN-10: 0-545-20273-6

Text copyright © 2006 by Holly Webb
Illustrations copyright © 2006 by Sophy Williams

All rights reserved. Published by Scholastic Inc.,
557 Broadway, New York, NY 10012.
SCHOLASTIC and associated logos are trademarks and/or registered
trademarks of Scholastic Inc.

Lexile is a registered trademark of MetaMetrics, Inc.

12 11 10 9 8 7 6 5 4 3 2 1   8 9 10 11 12 13/0

Printed in the China.
First Scholastic printing, November 2008

Chapter One

Rosebridge Farm was a beautiful place in autumn. The leaves on the big oak tree at the corner of the farmyard had turned golden, and every so often a few of them would whirl down to the ground and scare the hens. The farm was a lovely old place, and the Moffat family had been dairy farmers there for more than a hundred years.

There were stables, a big barn, and a beautiful old farmhouse that looked cozy and inviting in the autumn sunshine.

But today no one at the farm was noticing how lovely it all was. Mrs. Moffat and her son, Ben, were in the office, looking at the bills and worrying. It had been a difficult year, and money was tight.

Outside in the yard, Sara, Mrs. Moffat's thirteen-year-old daughter, was trying to give the henhouse a makeover. "Ow!" she yelped as she hit herself with the hammer for the fourth time. "Sorry, chicks," she said to the hens, who were scratching and pecking around her feet. "You're just going to have to wait for Ben to come and help me." She put down the hammer and headed off to the farmhouse, but as she passed the stables something made her stop.

What was that funny squeaking noise? Sara peered over the half-door at Gus, their old pony. He gazed back and snorted, shaking himself all over. Then he nosed down at a pile of straw practically underneath him. His face seemed to be saying that he wasn't complaining, but really, of all the places . . .

"Rosie! You've had the kittens!" exclaimed Sara excitedly. She leaned so far over the door, she nearly fell into the stable. Rosie, the farm cat, glared at her. "Sorry, sorry! I promise I won't come in and disturb you. I just want to have a quick look."

The kittens were snuggled up next to Rosie in Gus's bed of straw. They were tripping over one another as they nuzzled gently at their mother, still blind and helpless.

"Oh, they're gorgeous, Rosie! So how many are there? Two black ones, an orange tabby—oh no, two orange tabbies. I wish you'd hold still, kittens, I'm counting. And a brown tabby— oh. Oh, dear." Sara's delighted voice flattened. The brown tabby kitten was so tiny—much, much smaller than her brothers and sisters—and she was hardly moving.

"Oh, I hope you'll be all right!" Sara whispered worriedly as one of the others climbed over it. But she had a horrible

feeling that the tiny thing was just too small to survive. . . .

Even though Sara had lived on the farm all her life, and she knew that this sort of thing just happened sometimes, her eyes filled with tears.

The littlest kitten was so sweet—it had really long fur and looked like a little bundle of fluff! As she watched, it got stepped on again and opened its mouth in a tiny, almost silent mew of protest. Sara wiped her sleeve across her eyes sadly.

She took one last look at the kittens— at least the other four looked fit and healthy—and dashed off to tell her mom and Ben.

"Rosie's had her kittens!" she called as she opened the kitchen door.

Mrs. Moffat popped her head around the door of the office. "Oh, lovely! How many are there?"

"Five, but—"

"Five more mouths to feed," a gloomy voice sighed. Ben went to an agricultural college, training in farm management. He loved Rosebridge Farm, all the Moffats did, but he hated that things weren't going well. The farm was hardly making enough money to live on at the moment, and Ben was counting every penny.

"Oh, they're only tiny mouths, Ben! We can feed five little kittens!" His mother laughed.

"I think it might be only four soon," said Sara. "The little brown tabby one—it's so small. I'm not sure it'll make it."

"Oh, dear," said Mrs. Moffat, jumping up and coming out to the kitchen. "Let's take a look, Sara. Where are they?"

Sara led her mom and Ben out to see the new family, hoping that her mom would say she was making a fuss about nothing. But Mrs. Moffat looked at the littlest kitten sadly. "I think you might be right, Sara. It's too little. What a pity."

"Please don't call her an *it*, Mom. I'm sure she's a little girl kitten."

"I know what you mean. She's so pretty and delicate, with those lovely brown and black markings." Mrs. Moffat sighed.

"Isn't there anything we can do?" Sara

asked, tears filling her eyes again.

"Well, I suppose we could try giving her some of that special kitten milk out of an eyedropper," her mom said doubtfully. "That's if Rosie will let us. But Sara, you can't let yourself get too attached to her. I'm really sorry, but her chances just aren't good."

Over the next couple of weeks, Sara wondered if Rosie had heard them saying that the little kitten wasn't likely to survive. Rosie was a stubborn old cat, and she seemed determined to prove everyone wrong. She always made sure that the little one got an extra turn suckling, and by the time the kittens were three weeks old and starting to explore the stable, the littlest kitten was still little, but she was catching up. Rosie was very protective of them, but she did let Sara and her mom in to feed the brown tabby and cuddle them all every so often. The littlest kitten fought for more than her fair share of cuddles and would lie in Sara's arms, purring a purr that seemed far too loud for such a tiny creature.

It wasn't long before the bigger kittens got bored with exploring the stable and playing tag around Gus's hooves, and started trying to escape outside.

One morning the two orange tabby kittens hid behind the stable door. As soon as Sara opened it, they shot out into the farmyard. They seemed a bit surprised by how much world there was out there, but they certainly weren't going back in. Rosie seemed to realize that she couldn't keep them all shut up any longer, so she shooed the other kittens out, too. But the brown tabby cried and hid behind Rosie—outside was just too big and scary.

Rosie nudged the little kitten to the door, where she meowed miserably, her tiny paws scrabbling as she fought to get back into the safety of the cozy stable.

"Rosie, don't be such a bully!" said Sara, scooping up the trembling kitten. "Poor little ball of fluff, she's scared."

The kitten snuggled into Sara's

sweater—that was a much better place to be. And she'd heard that word *fluff* again. Everyone seemed to say it when

they saw her. *Perhaps Fluff is my name?* she thought happily.

Sara, Ben, and Mrs. Moffat had decided not to give any of the kittens names, as they knew that they wouldn't be at the farm for very long. As soon as the kittens were eight weeks old, they'd be old enough to leave Rosie and find new homes.

But it was hard not to call the little one Fluff. Sara gave in first, and Ben and her mom yelled at her about it.

"I told you not to get attached to any of them!" her mom scolded. "If you give her a name, you'll want her to stay, and you know we can't afford it."

"Eating us out of house and home as it is," muttered Ben, stroking the little kitten under the chin and trying not to grin as her massive purr rumbled around the stable.

"But she just is a Fluff!" cried Sara, grinning. "Look at her—she's the world's fluffiest kitten!"

It was true. And Fluff had beautiful markings, too: a fluffy brown-and-black tabby coat, huge white paws, and a white shirtfront. She'd inherited Rosie's dark brown eyes, and although she had a huge purr, her meow was still the same tiny little noise that had broken Sara's heart the day she'd been born.

It seemed no time at all before the kittens were eight weeks old. Fluff was still small compared to the others, and she looked even smaller because she seemed to be all fluff, whereas her brothers and sisters had short silky-smooth coats. Sara watched them as they played in the yard. The two black girl kittens were exploring an old bucket, while the two male orange tabbies played tug-of-war with a piece of string. As usual, Fluff sat on her own, watching her brothers and sisters, too timid to join in. Sara sighed. She couldn't help feeling sorry for the little kitten, who always seemed to be left out of their fun and games.

Mrs. Moffat and Ben appeared at the back door with steaming mugs of tea. "I know you'd like to keep them all, Sara, but I think the kittens are big enough to leave Rosie now," said Mrs. Moffat as she watched them playing. "I'll put up a sign on the gate, saying they're free to good homes. I can put up the signs for Christmas wreaths at the same time— making those always brings in extra money at this time of year. And we need every penny." She smiled.

Sara and Ben made faces. The farm was on the outskirts of Fairford, and lots of people came to buy holly wreaths and mistletoe at Christmas. The wreaths made a lot of money, but it meant spending December with prickled fingers.

"It's a pity," Ben said, watching Fluff

halfheartedly chase a piece of string. "I don't think anyone will want the little fluffy one—she's so skinny, she looks half-starved."

"How can you be so cruel—she's gorgeous!" Sara protested. But secretly, she couldn't help hoping Ben was right. Fluff was her favorite and she couldn't imagine her out there in the big wide world beyond the farm.

Chapter Two

Fluff and the other kittens knew that they would all be leaving to go to new homes soon. Whenever there were visitors, they had to be on their best behavior in the hope that someone might want to take them home. It had been the same with Rosie's last litter of kittens.

Fluff wasn't sure about it all. She loved

Rosebridge Farm. But then a home of her own did sound wonderful. Fluff's brothers and sisters were very excited and kept trying to sneak out when the gates were open.

Every time there was a customer for the lovely Christmas wreaths, Mrs Moffat would point out the kittens, frisking around cutely in the yard. It wasn't long before the two black girl kittens were snapped up by a lady who fell in love with them as they wove themselves around her legs.

It looked so easy, Fluff thought, and the next day she waited for a friendly looking customer and tried it for herself. But she tripped the man, and he stomped off with wet and muddy trousers.

The orange tabbies found owners a few days later, and Fluff watched them being carried away in a carrying case. She felt very alone. Rosie was still there, and Gus, and the hens, but it wasn't the same without her brothers and sisters. Even though they'd laughed at her, Fluff missed them. She took to sitting on top of Gus's half-door and moping.

Rosie tried to persuade her back down, but Fluff preferred to stay where she was. Rosie gave up eventually, but when they curled up in the hay to sleep that night, she was extra affectionate to Fluff, nuzzling her comfortingly. The big tabby cat wrapped her tail around her last little kitten and purred as she drifted off to sleep.

But Fluff lay awake, fretting. She thought that her mother was disappointed to have such a skinny, nervous kitten. What was going to happen to her? Mrs. Moffat kept looking at her worriedly, and Fluff couldn't help thinking, *What happens to kittens who nobody wants?*

A few days later, Fluff was perched up on Gus's door when a car drove up outside the farmyard. Fluff had given up trying to look lovable, as no one seemed to be interested in taking her home, so she stayed put and just watched.

A lady and her daughter had come to buy a holly wreath. The girl, who was about seven, ran around excitedly, eager to explore. She poked her head into the henhouse and climbed the fence to look at the cows. Then she began exploring the yard. Her mom kept calling her back— "Ella! Don't get in the way! Ella! Don't get your shoes muddy!"—but Ella wasn't listening.

Then she saw Fluff.

"Oh, what a pretty kitten! Please, can I stroke you? Kitty?"

A pretty kitten? Does she mean me? Fluff was so surprised that she turned around to see if there was another kitten behind her, forgetting how carefully she was balanced on top of the door. She meowed frantically and clawed her way back up again.

"I'm sorry, I didn't mean to scare you, poor little bundle of fluff."

Fluff looked at Ella in amazement. This girl knew her name! She reached out to the girl's hand and butted against it with her head, purring delightedly.

"Oh, aren't you sweet? Can I pick you up?" Ella asked gently.

She certainly could! Fluff snuggled into her neck and licked her chin, making Ella giggle. She tickled Fluff's bright white shirtfront. "The sign outside said they need homes for kittens. Maybe I could take you home? Mom and Dad promised I could have a pet soon, and you would be perfect!"

Fluff purred blissfully. Someone wanted to take her home! Someone who was very, very good at stroking.

Please take me home! she meowed.

Ella carried Fluff back over to her mother, who was paying Mrs. Moffat for the wreath.

"Oh, your little girl's found Fluff," said Mrs. Moffat hopefully. "We're looking for a home for her. I don't suppose you—"

"Ella! Put that grubby little kitten down!" said Ella's mother in horror.

Grubby? Fluff laid her ears back. She wasn't grubby, was she? She opened her eyes wide at Ella's mother and tried to look clean.

"Mom, she's not grubby, she's beautiful! Can't we take her home, please? She needs a home, and you did say I could have a pet soon."

"Yes, I know, but not a cat, Ella! A goldfish, maybe. Something nice and clean. And quiet."

"But I don't want a fish! I don't like fish. They're boring. You know I love cats, and Fluff's perfect. Please? I'll look after her."

"No, Ella, I'm sorry, but we don't want a cat in the house. Now come on, we've got Christmas shopping to do."

"Mom, please!" Ella begged.

"No! Now put her down."

Ella's eyes filled with tears, but she put Fluff down gently, kissing the top of her head.

"I'm sorry, Fluff. I'd love to take you home, I think you're beautiful." Ella gave the little brown tabby one last stroke.

Fluff couldn't believe it. She watched Ella leave, confused and meowing frantically. "Come back! Come back!" Someone had wanted her, wanted to give her a home. And now she was gone!

Chapter Three

That evening, Ella's mom was starting to wish that she'd never taken Ella to Rosebridge Farm. Ella had spent the rest of the day talking nonstop about Fluff, and when her dad arrived home from work, she didn't even give him the chance to take off his coat.

"Dad, you have to talk to Mom! You did say I could have a pet, didn't you? You promised! I found the best pet ever, and Mom says I can't have her, and you have to help me persuade her!"

Ella's dad sighed. He had a feeling that this was one of those situations where he was going to get into trouble whatever he said. "Um, have you? That's nice," he murmured cautiously.

"No, it isn't! Because Mom says I can't have her. You have to talk to her!"

Ella grabbed his arm and dragged him into the kitchen.

Ella's mom was reading a magazine. She had been ignoring Ella for the last hour, because however many times she explained that they couldn't have a cat, it didn't seem to be sinking in. She gave her husband a look that meant "Don't you dare!"

Ella's dad plunked himself down at the table and sighed. "Ella, I'm sorry, but I have no idea what you're talking about. Come sit down and tell me again."

Ella huffed irritably and grabbed the nearest chair. "You said I could have a pet. I've found the pet I want. So can I have her, please?" she pleaded.

Ella's dad took a deep breath. "Ella, you know there's more to it than that. Mom and I did say you could have a pet, but it's got to be the right kind of pet."

"But this is the right kind of pet! She's beautiful!"

"Um, what is she exactly?"

"A cat, of course! The prettiest kitten ever, Dad! She's got gorgeous big eyes, and great fat paws, and the fluffiest fur you've ever seen. And she's so tiny, and she really needs a home. Her name is Fluff. So can we go back to the farm and get her? Please?"

Ella's dad shook his head. "Ella, we said you could have a hamster! Maybe! If you were very good! Not a cat. We don't want a cat!"

Ella looked shocked. She'd been pinning all her hopes on her dad saying yes. "But why not?" she asked in a small voice. "She's such a sweet cat, Dad. You'd love her. Why don't you just come and see—"

"Ella, Dad said no!" her mom put in tiredly. "And I've already said no. You cannot have that cat, or any cat—"

"I don't want *any* cat! I want Fluff!" Ella said, her eyes tearing up.

She got up from the table and hurried up to her room. She couldn't believe that her parents had said no. Especially when poor Fluff needed a home so badly. What if no one ever came to take her home?

Chapter Four

The next morning, Fluff was still pining for Ella, in spite of Rosie's efforts to cheer her up.

She slunk out of the stable and batted a piece of paper backward and forward, occasionally summoning up the energy for a little pounce, but it didn't stop her from feeling miserable about Ella.

It wasn't long before a car pulled up on

the road outside the farm, and a woman and her son appeared in the yard. Fluff didn't take much notice, until she heard the woman asking about kittens.

Mrs. Moffat sounded delighted. "Actually, we've got just one left, but she's a dear little thing. She's there, look, playing with that piece of paper."

Mrs. Moffat came over and picked Fluff up, stroking her gently and murmuring nice things. Fluff began to purr, even though she still felt sad. How lovely it would be to have someone to pet her like that all the time! These people couldn't be as nice as Ella, but at least they would give her a home. She rubbed a damp paw quickly around her face and tried to look clean.

"Isn't she cute?" said the woman, tickling Fluff under her chin. "She'll make you a sweet pet, won't she, Nathan?" she said to the boy.

Nathan didn't look convinced. He just glared at Fluff.

"You see, we want Nathan to have a pet to teach him a sense of responsibility," Nathan's mother said to Mrs. Moffat. "He's been in a bit of trouble at school, and one of the teachers came up with the idea. A cat will be perfect."

Nathan spoke for the first time. "I don't want a cat. Cats are boring. Can't I have something cool, like a tarantula or a snake?"

"Don't be silly, Nathan," snapped his mother. "You know we all agreed on a cat."

Mrs. Moffat began to look doubtful, and Fluff laid her ears back at the sound of the angry voices. She wasn't sure she liked this family after all.

"You know, I'm not sure. . . . If your son doesn't really want Fluff, you might be better off—"

"Really, she'll be fine with us. Nathan will love her, once he gets used to the idea. Perhaps he could hold her?"

Mrs. Moffat looked worriedly at Nathan's scowl, but his mother gave him a look, and he seemed to remember his manners. "Please, can I hold her?" he asked politely.

Still slightly unsure, Mrs. Moffat handed him Fluff. Nathan held her as though he wasn't quite sure how to and patted the top of her head. Too hard—Fluff felt grateful she had nice, thick fur to protect her.

"See, isn't she sweet? You'll be friends in no time." Nathan's mother turned to Mrs. Moffat. "Could we take her now? Do you have a box or something that we could carry her home in?"

As soon as his mother and Mrs. Moffat had gone to look for a box, Nathan stopped being quite so nice. He held Fluff out at arm's length and made a disgusted face at her.

"I'm not taking care of you," he sneered. "Stupid, ratty little thing." He grabbed the scruff of her neck and poked her angrily. "I'll be stuck feeding you and everything. Even a dog would be better."

He made a growling noise. "Anyway, I won't have to bother for long. Our next door neighbor's German shepherd will have you for breakfast."

Fluff looked at the boy with huge round eyes. This was not going to be a home after all. If only she could just stay

here! But Mrs. Moffat had said all the kittens must go. She needed a real home. Somewhere with a friendly, loving person to take care of her. She needed Ella!

Fluff's fur stood up on end. She hissed angrily at Nathan, then sank a mouthful of sharp little teeth into the finger that he was prodding her with. He yelped and dropped her. Fluff landed lightly on the floor and took a flying leap onto the farmyard wall. She was going to do what Rosie had always forbidden. She took a last look at her old home, and then she jumped down the other side of the wall.

Mrs. Moffat and Nathan's mother came back into the yard just in time to see a fluffy tabby tail whisking over the wall, and Nathan looking shocked and guilty.

"Fluff!" Mrs. Moffat cried, running to the gate. She wrenched it open and dashed outside. But there was no little kitten waiting to be called back in, no flash of brown fur disappearing around the corner. Fluff was gone!

Chapter Five

On the other side of Fairford, Ella was lying on her bedroom floor, drawing a picture. It was a picture she'd drawn at least twenty times already. Sometimes Fluff was sitting down, sometimes she was walking along the stable door, but she always looked sad. Sad and lonely, just like Ella was feeling. Ella got out her best watercolor pencils and started to color in Fluff's lovely tabby fur, using a wet paintbrush to make it look soft and fluffy. How could her mom say Fluff was grubby? She was so beautiful! Ella carefully outlined Fluff's big eyes with black and added her sparkling white whiskers and eyebrows. Then she got out her gel pens and added a little silver tear trickling out of the corner of each eye.

"Ella, there you are." Ella hadn't even

noticed her dad calling her. It was Saturday, and he'd been out in the yard trimming the Christmas tree, preparing to bring it indoors. "That's beautiful. Is that Fluff?"

Ella nodded and sniffed, and then a real tear splashed down onto the paper and made Fluff's fur run. It was ruined. Ella blinked back the tears and sadly scrunched up the piece of paper. She'd given up arguing with her parents about Fluff, because it wasn't doing any good, but she couldn't stop being miserable and worrying about the little kitten.

"Ella, will you come downstairs for a minute? Your mom and I want to talk to you."

Ella sighed, but followed her dad downstairs. She knew what they were going to say. Mom and Dad were going to try to cheer her up again like they had earlier. So far, they'd suggested Christmas shopping, decorating the Christmas tree, and a trip to *The Nutcracker*. But even though *The Nutcracker* had been a fantastic treat, Ella just couldn't stop thinking about Fluff.

Her parents were sitting at the kitchen table, looking serious. Ella's mom took her hand. "Ella, your dad and I know you've been really sad about not being able to have Fluff. We've talked it over, and although we're still a bit worried about it, we've decided that you can have her after all—"

Ella didn't wait to hear more. She threw herself at her mom, knocking the breath out of her. "You mean it? Thank you, thank you, thank you!"

"Ella, listen. You can only have Fluff

on the condition that you take good care of her. She'll need feeding twice a day, and grooming, especially if she's as fluffy as you say she is. You'll have to be very responsible." Dad's voice was serious, and Ella nodded.

"I'll take good care of her, I promise." Ella was beaming. She would do anything!

"Well, what are we waiting for?" Dad bounced up from the table. "Let's go get her! Why don't we walk over to the farm? It's only a short walk to the other side of town, and it's a beautiful day."

Ella dashed into the hall and put on her pink sheepskin boots and fluffy winter jacket. She added a hat with earflaps and a huge scarf.

Dad laughed. "You're right, it's freezing out there. I wouldn't be surprised if it snowed soon. Now, where are my gloves?"

Ella was dancing around with impatience by the time her mom and dad were ready. Dad went next door to borrow their cat carrier, and he laughed at Ella's jittery face. "Well, what were you thinking, that you'd just tuck her inside that scarf of yours?" Ella thought that sounded perfect. Finally they were ready to go, walking through town, weaving their way around the bustling shoppers. It was beautiful—with Christmas only four days away, everyone was in a festive mood, and all the shopwindows were full of presents, tinsel, and sparkling Christmas trees.

Ella held her dad's hand, rushing him along. "She's such a pretty kitten, Dad, you'll love her. I'll take really good care of her, I promise. Oh, look, there's the sign for the farm. Come on! I can't wait to see her again!"

Ella ran the last little way, and her mom and dad exchanged smiles. They hadn't been sure about letting Ella have a kitten, but she was so happy, it had to be the right decision.

They opened the farm gate, and Ella dashed off to try to find Fluff, while her parents went to look for Mrs. Moffat.

"Fluff! Fluff!" Ella called, but no little kitten came running. There was a beautiful big tabby cat sitting quietly on the stable door, just where Fluff had been when Ella first saw her. Ella went over to her. "You must be Fluff's mom! You have to be, your eyes are just the same. Where is she? We've come to take her home!"

The tabby cat gave Ella a long look, then jumped down from the door and disappeared around the corner of the yard, walking very fast. It was almost as if Ella had upset her.

Just then Ella's mom and dad came out of the farmhouse with Mrs. Moffat. "I'm really sorry," she was explaining. "It's such bad luck—really awful timing."

"Oh, no! Has someone else taken Fluff home?" Ella gasped.

"N-no—not exactly," said Mrs. Moffat, looking worried. "I'm afraid Fluff is lost. Some people came to see about taking her earlier this morning, and I think the boy frightened her. She jumped over the wall and disappeared. She's never even been out of the gate before! I've been searching all around, and so have Ben and Sara, but we can't find her anywhere. It's odd; she's normally such a friendly little thing, I'd have expected her to come running. We'll keep looking, of course, but—"

Ella's dad could see that Ella was about to burst into tears, and he put his arm around her. "If you find her, could you let us know?" he asked. He scribbled their phone number on a bit of paper and handed it to Mrs. Moffat.

"Can't we go look for her?" Ella begged as they left the farm. "We might find her."

"Ella, she could be a long way away by

now," her mom explained. "Mrs. Moffat's already looked all around here. I'm afraid we don't have much chance of finding her."

"But she's so little! And Mrs. Moffat said she's never been outside the farm before." Ella started to cry, and her dad hugged her tight.

"Mrs. Moffat's going to keep looking. You never know . . ."

Ella nodded miserably and shivered. It was so cold. Poor Fluff was out here lost and all alone. How would such a little kitten ever find her way home?

Chapter Six

The minute Fluff had landed on the other side of the wall, she'd set off as fast as her legs would carry her. She wanted to get as far away as possible from that horrible boy and, without knowing it, she'd run into one of the town's main streets, which was packed with Christmas shoppers. Now Fluff was cowering behind a garbage can, watching shoes, all of which were threatening to step on her. She'd been sitting there for ages. She'd never imagined that outside could be so big. There were so many people, and so many cars roaring past. No wonder Rosie had warned them to stay in the yard! She had no idea what she should do next. How on earth was she going to find Ella? Cautiously, she put a paw out of her hiding place, and then whipped it back quickly as another boot came down and nearly squashed it. She squeezed herself back behind the trach can and sat there shivering.

Fluff felt like she'd been under there for hours when she finally dared to come out. She felt safer now that it was dark and there were fewer people around. She sniffed the air hopefully. Food smells were all around, but she had no idea where they were coming from. Back at the farm she would have been fed by now, and her stomach rumbled loudly. She slunk along the edges of the sidewalk, hiding in the shadows, until finally the shops gave way to houses and yards. Then she jumped up onto a wall to give herself a view of the street, and settled down to rest and think about what to do next.

All at once, she missed the cozy stable and the comforting sound of Gus the pony snorting in his sleep. *Oh, why did I ever leave the farm?* Fluff meowed. Then she shook her whiskers firmly. *Because I'm going to find Ella, that's why,* she told herself.

Suddenly she was jolted out of her thoughts by an angry hissing. She spun around at once, her fur fluffing up. A huge tomcat was towering over her, his tail flailing to and fro and his whiskers bristling.

Fluff gasped. He seemed to be at least three times as big as she was! She meowed hopefully at him. Perhaps he could show her where to find some food. Ducking her head shyly, she crept along the wall toward him.

The tomcat was anything but friendly. He made a low growling noise as he inched toward her. Then, in one quick movement, he lifted one of his enormous paws and cuffed Fluff around the head, sending her flying. Dazed, Fluff landed badly on the sidewalk below. She shot off down the street, looking back just once, to see the massive cat hulking on the wall and staring after her.

Fluff didn't stop running until she was at least three streets away. She sneaked under a gate into a garden and wriggled herself under a bush, her heart thumping. She was only a kitten, and she had no idea about life outside the farm. How was she to know that the wall belonged to the tomcat? Did everywhere outside belong to somebody else? She tried to snuggle down into the old dead leaves under the bush, but she couldn't relax, and she spent the rest of the night dozing, and then waking in a panic every time she heard a rustle of leaves or the squawk of a night bird. *I shouldn't have run away*, Fluff thought. *Even that boy couldn't be as bad as this. Could he?*

Only a few streets away, Ella's parents were sitting in their warm kitchen drinking tea together. Ella's mom frowned. "I really don't know what to do to cheer her up." She sighed. "It's not that she's being sulky, or difficult, or anything like that—she just seems so sad."

Ella's dad nodded. "What's really upset her is that Fluff's out there lost and all alone. Ella's frightened for her."

"And I have a horrible feeling that Mrs. Moffat won't be able to find her," worried Ella's mom. "I know I didn't really want Ella to have a cat, but it's so sad that it's turned out like this. It's so cold out there now, and—goodness, what was that? Did you hear a noise out in the hall?"

They jumped up from the table and hurried out of the kitchen.

"Ella! What on earth are you doing? You're supposed to be in bed!"

Ella was standing on a pile of books, trying to undo the security chain on the front door. She was wearing her pajamas tucked into her purple galoshes, and her eyes were blotchy from crying.

"I've got to find Fluff!" she said desperately, fumbling with the chain. "Can we go out and look for her?" The streetlight was casting strange blue and green shadows through the stained-glass panels in the door, and Ella looked like a little ghost.

"Ella, it's ten o'clock! And it's freezing

outside!" Ella's mom started to help her down from her makeshift ladder.

"I know!" Ella wailed. "But Fluff's out there, Mom, all on her own. Please let me go out and look for her!"

"Ella, you can't go out there in the dark," said her dad firmly. "Anyway, someone else might have found Fluff; she could be fine. But I promise I'll take you out looking for her tomorrow. And Mom will call the farm and see if they've had any more news." He tightened the security chain carefully. "That's only if you go straight back to bed now."

Ella cast one longing look back at the door and reluctantly sat down on the stairs to take off her galoshes. "You promise?"

"Definitely. We'll do our best to find her, just not now."

Ella nodded and trailed sadly back up the stairs, carrying her books.

Chapter Seven

Fluff woke with a start to find that it was getting light. She shivered as she remembered why she wasn't curled up in the cozy stable with Rosie. She stretched painfully, stiff with cold, and started on a quick morning wash. It was while she was busy with the delicate job of cleaning behind her ears that she realized what the strange feeling in her middle must be. She hadn't had anything to eat since yesterday's breakfast, and she was starving! She needed to find some food very soon. She could smell that there were mice around, but she didn't think she had much chance of catching one. But that garbage can she'd found shelter behind yesterday had had food smells coming from it. She set off out of the garden to find a trash can.

It wasn't long before she came to a waste basket attached to a lamppost. Fluff sniffed hopefully—it had a definite foody whiff. It took several tries, but after a flying leap and a lot of scrabbling, Fluff found herself balanced on the edge of the can, catching her breath. She took a deep sniff—cheese! Sara had occasionally given her a nibble of cheese from her sandwiches, and there was definitely cheese in this can. There was another odd smell as well, a little like mouse, but Fluff wasn't quite sure what it was.

Fluff leaned over, balancing as carefully as she could. Yes, there it was! Half a cheese sandwich! She reached out a delicate paw and hooked it out triumphantly. She was just about to jump down and drag the sandwich away somewhere quiet when there was a sudden scuffling noise underneath her, and the garbage moved.

An enormous rat popped up from under a hamburger box and bared his dirty big teeth at Fluff. Then he snatched the sandwich back and hissed at her.

Fluff lost her balance and slid off

backward, twisting frantically in the air, but still landing painfully and jarring her paws. She raced off down the street, sure she could still hear the rat's horrible hissing in her ear.

At last, out of breath, and with her

paws aching, she scuttled under a parked car to hide. *What am I going to do?* she panicked. *I can't find anywhere safe to sleep, or anything to eat, and I can't find Ella! Maybe I should just go back?* She missed Rosie, and Gus the pony, and everyone at the farm. And right this minute, she really missed the food and her warm bed in the stable!

The farm was the only home she'd ever known, and all she had to do was go back the way she'd come. Surely that boy would be gone by now. *Maybe they'll be glad to see me back,* she thought. *They might even let me stay!* She set off, retracing her steps, but crossed to the other side of the road and ran to avoid the garbage can and the scary rat. Those first few streets weren't too hard, but when Fluff got back to the garden where she'd slept under a bush, nothing looked familiar. Which way had she come from? Where was the tomcat's wall? Fluff shivered with cold. She looked down the road one way and then the other. She hadn't a clue—but it was getting so cold and she had to make a decision. She set off again, hoping that she would come across something that she remembered. But a few streets later Fluff found herself trotting past a little row of shops that she was certain she'd never seen before. She paused on the edge of the sidewalk to try and figure out when she'd made her mistake.

Suddenly, there was a loud roaring

noise and a car shot past her, skidding through a deep, muddy puddle and soaking Fluff to the skin in dirty water. She gasped in shock as she felt the cold biting into her. She shuddered and looked around desperately for a warm place to dry off.

A lady with a big shopping bag was going into one of the shops, and Fluff felt the gust of warmth as the door opened. *Surely they wouldn't mind if I just went in to get warm,* she thought. *I won't stay long.*

The shop was brightly lit, and it looked so inviting that Fluff couldn't resist. She hurried over and followed the lady in, sneaking along behind her shopping bag.

It was so nice to be somewhere warm again! She peeked around the side of the bag and gulped with delight. There was a bowl of food at the corner of the counter! Fluff didn't stop to think. She darted over to the bowl and started to gobble as fast as she could.

She'd managed a few mouthfuls, when a strange *rrrrr*-ing noise made the fur on the back of her neck lift up. She froze in panic, her heart thumping. There wasn't a dog on the farm, and Fluff had never met one before, but some deep cat instinct stirred inside her.

The *rrrrr*-ing changed to a deep woof, and suddenly an enormous creature flung itself at Fluff, barking madly and baring its teeth.

The lady with the bag and the shop owner looked down in amazement. "What's the matter with you, Fergus, you silly dog? Oh, my goodness! Where did that scrawny little thing come from? And it's stealing your dinner! Shoo, you nasty stray. Go on, Fergus, chase it out, it's probably full of fleas!" The man flung the door open and Fergus (who was only a small dog, but thought he was at least a Great Dane) chased Fluff out onto the sidewalk, his teeth inches from her tail.

When Fluff dared to look back, she was surprised to see that the dog wasn't actually much bigger than she was. It wasn't fair! Why shouldn't she have had some of that nice food, too? There had been plenty for them both. She skidded to a stop and spat angrily at Fergus. She was sick of running away. She stood nose to nose with the little dog and hissed, her tail twitching. Then, as he started to bark again, she shot out a paw and raked her tiny claws down his muzzle.

Fergus howled in shock. The little cat was supposed to run off shaking like jelly, not fight back! He wailed again, and his owner, who'd been watching from the door, flung a newspaper at Fluff, yelling, "Get out of here, you horrible stray!"

Fluff dodged the newspaper, but the man's words hit her. She'd been too busy running the first time he'd called her a stray, but now it struck home. She slunk off into the shadows, feeling more alone than ever. She was a stray!

She knew all about strays. No one wanted them, and Rosie chased them away if they came to the farm. If Fluff was a stray cat now, maybe she wouldn't be welcome at the farm after all . . . .

Chapter Eight

Fluff padded sadly along the sidewalk. She was a little less hungry after the food she'd stolen from Fergus's bowl, but she was still frozen. It was already getting dark again, and it seemed even colder than the night before. Fluff decided to look for somewhere to hide for the night and think about what to do in the morning. She trotted down a dark alleyway with a row of trash cans down one side.

The alley was full of good smells, but about halfway down Fluff noticed another smell that somehow wasn't so good. In fact, it was almost a scary smell. She took a deep sniff, trying to work out what it was. It was a little bit like the smell of Fergus, but not quite. Stronger and—dirtier, somehow . . . She lifted her head, sensing that someone was watching her, and gulped.

A huge fox was peering at her around the nearest trash can, his tongue lolling and a hungry gleam in his eye. He had Fluff cornered, and they both knew it.

Fluff froze in panic for a second. He was enormous!

Then she shot backward and squeezed

herself into a tiny space between two
cans, where the fox wouldn't be able to
get to her. Did foxes eat kittens? Fluff
wasn't sure, but this one was looking at

her as though she might make a tasty snack. He stuck his nose into Fluff's hiding spot, eyeing her all the while. He reached a paw in, and then his shoulder, and then he banged one of the cans out of the way, knocking it over. He grinned at Fluff, showing his enormous teeth.

Fluff was trapped, but she wasn't giving up. She'd fought off Fergus, hadn't she? She fluffed up her fur and hissed defiantly, as much to make herself feel brave as anything else. The fox crept closer, and Fluff batted at him angrily with one tiny paw. It was like hitting a rock. This was no Fergus, about to turn tail. But there was nothing else she could do. . . .

Fluff hissed and spat as well as she knew how and, amazingly, after a few seconds the fox stopped. He seemed confused. He put his head to one side and watched her, a puzzled look in his eyes. Then, slowly, he started to make a strange barking noise and crouched down with his long muzzle resting on his paws.

Fluff gazed at him, confused and scared. What was he doing? It sounded almost like—was he laughing at her? She edged as far back as she could into the shelter of the cans, not sure what to do next. The fox watched, his nose still on his paws, and gave an encouraging yap. Then he wriggled backward on his haunches, giving her a clear space to escape.

Fluff watched, puzzled. Was he not going to eat her after all? He looked almost friendly. Suddenly, the fox sprang

up, and Fluff squashed herself backward against the wall, trembling. But instead of launching himself at the can, the fox turned tail and disappeared down the alley. Fluff waited a moment, then poked her nose gingerly out of her hiding place and peered around. The fox was coming back, his white-tipped tail waving jauntily, and in his mouth was a piece of ham. It was chewed and smelly, but it looked delicious. Fluff's whiskers twitched with longing.

The fox laid the ham down in front of Fluff and retreated.

Was this a trap? Was he going to pounce as soon as she was out of her shelter? Fluff eyed the ham and tried to measure the distances. But her tummy was telling her to forget being careful and go for the food! She darted swiftly out, grabbed the ham, and ran back to the cans. The fox just watched, making that odd barking noise again. He hadn't even tried to catch her. Maybe he was friendly? Fluff shivered. This was the first friendly creature she'd met since she left the farm. It seemed strange that it should be a huge, scary fox.

The fox disappeared again, and Fluff

watched eagerly this time. Was he going to get more food? The fox trotted back, carefully holding something in his mouth. He set it down gently and pushed it toward her—a half-full can of tuna! This time Fluff didn't hesitate. The smell of the fish was too good to resist. The fox watched admiringly as Fluff wolfed it down, licking the edges of the can to catch the last morsels.

As Fluff licked the delicious juice from her whiskers, a huge yawn overtook her, and she stretched. Now that she wasn't so hungry, she realized how tired she was. But she still had nowhere to sleep.

The fox watched her thoughtfully, head to one side. Then he gave an encouraging yap and jerked his head. Fluff looked back cautiously. He seemed to want her to follow him. She wasn't sure whether it was safe, but she was just so tired. Perhaps the fox was going to show her somewhere she could rest. She set off after the fox, too sleepy to worry anymore. He led her off down the alley, looking back every so often to nod and twitch his ears at her.

They wiggled under a fence—it was much easier for Fluff than it was for the fox—and into an overgrown yard. The fox threaded his way through the brambles and then stood back proudly. He'd brought her to his den! It was a comfy hole under a garden shed, and it smelled horribly of fox. But Fluff was in no position to be choosy. The fox gave her a gentle nudge with his long nose, and she crept inside, snuggling down into an old sack. The fox looked in after her, as if to check that she was all right, and then trotted off. Fluff guessed he was going to find his own food.

Despite the smell, Fluff slept until it was light. Then she woke and stretched sleepily, confused for a moment about where she was. Of course! The fox's hole! And it looked as though he'd left her a snack. Lying by her nose was a piece of old sardine. Fluff nibbled it gratefully, still wondering why the fox had turned out to be so friendly. She stuck her nose out from under the shed and sniffed the fresh morning air. It was a nice change after the foxy odor of the den. After a good rest, and something to eat, Fluff was feeling much better. She was sure she would find Ella today. She wished the fox had come back so she could say good-bye, but there was no sign of him.

But if I don't find Ella, she thought, *I'll have no trouble finding my way back to see the fox again. I'll just follow the smell!*

Chapter Nine

"So, no news?" Ella's mom said into the phone. Ella sat on the kitchen counter beside her, trying to hear what Mrs. Moffat was saying. "No, it's awful, isn't it? Ella and her dad went out yesterday looking for Fluff, all around the town. They were out for hours, but they didn't even find anyone who'd spotted her. Well, thanks for trying, and do let us know if you hear anything." She put the phone down. "They haven't seen her, I'm afraid. Don't look so sad, Ella, someone else might have found her! She could be having a nice breakfast right this minute. Which reminds me—eat some of yours."

"I'm not hungry," Ella said sadly as she started pushing her Rice Krispies around the bowl. "Can we go out and put up the posters I made of Fluff?"

"Yes. *After* you've eaten your breakfast," her mother added.

Ella started to shovel in her cereal as fast as she could.

"And assuming you haven't choked to death on a Rice Krispie." Her mother sighed.

They walked over toward the farm to start with, and then came back along the main street. It was another freezing-cold day, and even Ella was starting to tire after an hour of sticking posters of Fluff onto every lamppost they could find. They all said the same thing:

Several people stopped to look and say

Lost
Long-haired
Tabby kitten
answers to the
name of FLUFF

how cute the little kitten was, but no one had seen her. When they got to the playground a few streets from their house, Ella's mom persuaded her to call it a day. "Lots of people will see all those posters. We need to get back home before we freeze. Come on, we'll go home and have some hot chocolate to warm us up. And then you promised to help me sort out all that old junk in the garage, remember?"

Ella nodded sadly. She'd really hoped that they would spot Fluff, but there'd been no sign of her. Ella tucked the roll of tape back into her pocket and put her gloves on. Her hands were going numb, and she shivered. Poor little Fluff. Mom and Dad kept saying that someone had probably found her by now, but what if she was still out in the cold?

Fluff was outside, and she was frozen. She'd left the fox's den that morning feeling very confident, but an hour later, she was running out of energy. She plodded on, her paws starting to feel tired again, and then, at the end of the road, she heard a noise that gave her some hope. She broke into a run and rounded the corner, following the laughter and yells to a playground. A group of children, all wearing winter coats and scarves, were rushing around to keep warm.

Fluff crouched down by the gate, searching the faces for Ella, but there was no sign of her. As she watched, still more children arrived. It seemed that every child in the neighborhood was coming and going from the playground. So surely Ella would come there, too? She settled herself under one of the benches near the edge of the playground and prepared to keep watch.

Some of the children tried to coax her out, but she wouldn't come. One little girl reached under to pat her, but her mother grabbed her and scolded her. "Leave it, Lucy, it's a stray. Look how dirty and matted its fur is. Don't encourage it!"

Several times she got up, ready to rush

over to some dark-haired girl bundled up in a coat and hat, then realized at the last minute that it wasn't Ella. But it wasn't until it began to get dark, and the parents sitting around waiting for their children started to call them to go home, that Fluff was forced to give up. She'd felt sure she'd find Ella here—she'd never seen so many children before. She left the playground, following the last of the children, and wandered down the road, trying to think what to do. She didn't know that there was a poster with her picture pinned to every lamppost.

She was hungry again, and thirsty, so she slipped under a gate and started to look around. The third yard she came to had a birdbath. Fluff leaped up onto the edge and dipped her tongue in. The water was freezing—really freezing. The edges of the birdbath were icing over! Fluff shivered as she felt the icy water settling in her tummy, and then jumped as something cold landed on her nose. Snow! Fluff had never seen it before, but Rosie had told her about it. She jumped down onto the grass. Fluff couldn't resist jumping and batting at the thick white flakes for a while, but the snow was falling fast and soon her paws were soaked.

Fluff looked uncertainly toward the nearby house. The windows were brightly lit, and she watched as two children hung tinsel around the pictures on the walls. There was a plump black cat with them, perched comfortably on the back of the sofa. Fluff could almost hear it purring. She jumped up onto the windowsill, which was already coated with a layer of snow, and pressed herself against the glass, desperate to be inside the warm room. The little boy went out and came back with a sandwich, which he shared with the black cat!

Fluff could hardly bear to watch, and she meowed piteously, hoping he would notice her and let her have some, too. But no one heard her. Then the children started a game, wafting the tinsel around

for the cat to chase, but all it did was yawn
and put out a paw occasionally.

I'll chase it, Fluff meowed. *I'll really*

chase it for you! But still they paid no attention, and then their mother came in and drew the curtains to shut out the dark and cold. No one saw the little brown cat huddled on the windowsill, crying to be let in.

Fluff jumped down and set off again. She needed to find shelter out of the snow. In the short time she'd spent on the windowsill, those few flakes of snow had thickened to a storm, and the snow already covered her paws as she plodded wearily through it. *I'll find a shed to hide under until this stops*, she decided. But none of the sheds she found had space to wriggle underneath them like her fox friend's den. She tried hiding behind some garbage cans along the side of a house, but the wind whistled straight through, and it was almost colder than out in the open.

She ducked underneath another fence and trekked across the next yard. The house was brightly lit, and the lamplight shining through the curtains cast pretty shadows through the blue and green stained glass in the door. *There's probably another fat black cat in there,* Fluff thought sadly. *Probably having a snack.* There were cardboard boxes by the garage, all piled up. One was full of old newspapers, and Fluff looked at it thoughtfully. It wasn't a great place to take shelter, but there wasn't much snow on it, and the newspapers did look so comfortable . . . Perhaps she could just have a little rest?

She clambered in, her legs feeling

awkward and clumsy with the cold, and curled up, a tiny ball of damp fur. She hadn't meant to go to sleep, but she was so tired. The snow kept falling, and it wasn't long before even the tips of Fluff's ears were covered. But by then, Fluff had fallen into a deep, cold sleep. . . .

Chapter Ten

Ella had been watching for her dad from the window for nearly an hour by the time he came home.

"Sorry I'm late, sweetheart. There was lots to finish up before the Christmas vacation," he explained as he hugged her.

"Did you see her, Dad? While you were driving home, did you see Fluff?"

"No, Ella, I'm sorry. You didn't have any luck when you went out looking with Mom today?"

"No." Ella shook her head sadly. "We went all around, as far as the playground, but we didn't see her. We put LOST posters up everywhere, too, with pictures I drew of Fluff on them."

"Well, we'll go out and look again tomorrow. It's Christmas Eve, and I'll be home all day. Good thing, too—the snow's getting quite deep out there."

Ella's mom called from the kitchen, "Is that you, Dave? Don't take your shoes off yet!"

Ella's dad sighed. "What is it? Can't it wait until tomorrow? It's freezing out there! Can't I have a cup of tea and sit down?" he called.

"No, because then I'll never get you up again! Ella and I sorted out all that recycling in the garage this afternoon; it took us ages. And now it's outside the garage getting snowed on! Can you put it in the car for me, so we're ready the next time we go past the recycling center?"

"Okay, okay," Ella's dad grumbled. He wound his scarf back around his neck and stepped out into the cold. He hurried over to the pile of boxes, leaving deep footprints in the snow. "They're full of snow already," he called back to Ella, who was peering around the door. "And heavy—ugh!" He picked up one of the boxes and struggled down the path to the car, balancing it on one knee while he unlocked the trunk. It took a few trips, but at last he headed back to the house, looking forward to a nice hot cup of tea.

Ella sat at the kitchen table, watching him drink it and looking hopeful. "Ella,

it's no use giving me that look. I'm not taking you out to search for Fluff again now. It's dark!"

"But Dad, you said the snow's getting deep! What if poor Fluff's buried in it?"

Her dad sighed. "Ella, I'm sorry, but if that's the case, then we wouldn't be able to find her, would we? I'm sure someone else will have found her by now. You put up the posters, so maybe whoever found her will get in touch." He knew that actually wasn't very likely, but he wanted to cheer her up. "You know what? I just remembered that I've got a surprise for you in the car. Come and see!"

"What's the surprise, Dad?" Ella asked as they trekked down the path, trying hard to sound excited. But he only smiled and wouldn't tell her. "Look on the backseat."

As she opened the car door and peered into the backseat, she heard an odd rustling sound from the trunk. "Dad? Does my surprise make a noise?"

"What, sweetheart?" Ella's dad was stamping his feet to keep warm.

"There was a funny noise from the trunk. Is it the surprise?"

"There's nothing in the trunk except those boxes of newspapers and things that you and your mom sorted out. It was probably just some snow falling off the roof or something."

"I'm sure it came from the trunk," Ella said doubtfully. She climbed in and peered over the backseat but the cargo cover was fixed in the way. The rustling sound came again, and Ella jumped, bumping her head on the car roof. "Ow! Dad, I heard it again! There is something in the trunk, honest." Ella wriggled out backward, feeling a bit nervous. "There's something moving around! Do you have a flashlight?"

"Well, there's a flashlight in the glove compartment, but really, Ella, there's nothing there!" He reached into the front of the car and poked around for the flashlight. "There you go."

Back in the trunk, Fluff was stirring. Ella's dad had had the heater on while he was driving home from work, and the car was still quite warm. Warmer than Fluff had been all day. She stretched blissfully in her sleep, and the melting snow slid off her, just as Ella opened the trunk and shone the flashlight inside.

"Wh—! Fluff! Oh, Dad, look, Fluff's in the box! That's the surprise; you've found Fluff! But you told me you hadn't seen her!"

"What? I haven't! My surprise was a big box of chocolates!" Her dad looked

confused. "Are you sure?" He peered into the trunk. "Well, that's definitely a kitten. . . . How on earth did she get there? You're sure that's Fluff?"

"I'm sure! Oh, Dad, she came to find us, and she went to sleep in the box!" Gently, Ella reached in and lifted the snoozing kitten out. "Oh, she's all wet and freezing! We have to get her dry."

Ella's dad shook his head. "I can't believe she came looking for you. Come on, let's get her inside."

They rushed back to the house and into the kitchen. Ella's mom was cooking dinner and didn't turn around. "So what was the surprise? Chocolates, perhaps? I'd love some chocolate."

"Oh! We left them in the car!" Ella

giggled, sounding happy for the first time in days. "Sorry, Mom!"

"Hmm, and I've got a complaint, Jen. You said you'd sorted through all that recycling," said Ella's dad, grinning. "Those bins are for bottles and paper only, you know. No kittens allowed."

"What?" Ella's mom spun around and saw Fluff cuddled in Ella's arms. "Oh! I don't believe it! Is that really Fluff? Where was she?"

"In the pile of newspapers, in the trunk of the car!"

Fluff was staring blearily around, wondering if she was still dreaming. But the soft towel that the girl was rubbing her with seemed to be real, and the girl really was Ella! She managed a small purr as warmth started to seep into her bones.

"We don't have any cat food," said Ella's mom worriedly, opening the

kitchen cupboard. "Do you think she'd like tuna?" she said, holding out a can to Ella. Fluff recognized it at once and stood up shakily on Ella's lap, meowing hopefully.

"Hmm, well, I'd better find the can opener." Ella's mom shook her head in amazement. "I can't believe we found her!"

"She found us, Mom! It's like a Christmas wish come true." Ella smiled to herself, stroking Fluff's ears. *And we're Fluff's Christmas present*, she thought. *Fluff's got a home for Christmas.*

"We should call the farm and let them know," Ella's dad said as he searched for an old bowl to put Fluff's tuna in.

"But what if they want her back?" Ella gasped in horror and hugged Fluff tightly, making her squeak. "Sorry, Fluff!"

"Don't worry, Ella. I'm sure they'll be delighted for you to keep her. They know how much you wanted Fluff and that you'll take good care of her." Her mom crouched down next to her and tickled Fluff under the chin. "You're right, she's not grubby, she's gorgeous!" She grinned at Ella, remembering the first time she'd seen Fluff. "We just don't want everyone at the farm to worry anymore, that's all. Mrs. Moffat wanted a good home for Fluff, and now she's got one."

Ella nodded, relieved. "And you'd better remind Mrs. Moffat to tell Fluff's mom she's safe. She was really worried." She saw her mom and dad exchange an amused look over her head, but she didn't care. Fluff was home, and nothing else mattered. And Fluff, digging into the big bowl of tuna, thought so, too.

Lost in the Storm

by Holly Webb
Illustrated by Sophy Williams

Ella loves her kitten, Fluff, and
worries about her going missing again.
But Fluff enjoys the freedom of being
outside, especially when it starts
snowing and she has pretty snowflakes
to play with and lots of wintry gardens
to explore.

But suddenly a blizzard sets in and
Fluff can't find her way home. Will
Ella ever be reunited with her kitten?

Animal Rescue

by Tina Nolan

Abandoned . . . lost . . . neglected . . . ?
There's always a home at Animal Magic!
In a perfect world there'd be no need
for Animal Magic. But Eva and Karl
Harrison, who live at the animal
rescue center with their parents, know
that life isn't perfect. Every day there's
a new arrival in need of their help!

Charlie

The Home-Alone Kitten

Everything's going well for Animal Magic's
Open Day, until the celebrity guest, soccer
star Jake Adams, cancels at the last minute.
Eva turns detective, but when she arrives at
Jake's house all she finds is his orange tabby
kitten, Charlie, locked out and meowing
on the doorstep. . . .

Honey
The Unwanted Puppy

When Eva finds Honey, a beautiful golden retriever puppy, dumped on the doorstep of Animal Magic, she's desperate to find the lovable dog a new home. But Karl has other ideas—he wants to follow up the clue to find Honey's real owner. . . .

Merlin
The Homeless Foal

When Merlin the foal is born at Animal Magic, Eva is desperate for him to find a home nearby. But it seems as if he will be moved to a farm too far away for her to visit. And that's not all Eva has to worry about: Mrs. Brooks's plan to close down the rescue center looks set to become reality. . . .

Rusty
The Injured Fox Cub

When Eva discovers an injured fox cub down by the river, she's desperate to nurse it back to health. Eva can't help picking him up and cuddling him, even though her mom has warned her that Rusty isn't a pet. Has Eva's love ruined Rusty's chance of being returned to the wild?